RENOVATE YOUR WORLD

SAKSHI GOYAL

Renovate your world; The Book

Authored by:

Sakshi Goyal

Renovate your world; The Book

Acknowledgment:

Hey, this is Sakshi Goyal, a charming, hardworking, and fun-loving girl. I believe in God like anyone else. I believe in quotations because these help us get some sort of motivation, so I had this hobby to write and collect quotations. I found it intriguing and worthy enough to be written somewhere, my random thoughts always inspired me to keep doing things that I like. I started writing and collecting these quotations back in 2011. Most of my quotations were posted by me on social media like Facebook and Instagram. Since my father, an advocate by Profession, Mr. Rajesh Kumar Gupta is turning 60 this year, I wished to dedicate him a book of my quotations, so I deliberately started working on compiling all new and old and gold ones into a piece of the full-fledged book and got in touch with few publishers like Black Cat Publication, and Legal Research and Analysis to further solidify my wishes to dedicate a book to my beloved father. He Has been an awe-inspiring father, he has done what any father would do for their daughter, He went on sending his daughter out of the city on her own for educational purposes, oh yeah by the way I have a master's in management without standing grace and secured 10 CGPA in 10th and 9.0 in my Senior secondary schooling from a convent school of Aligarh. I would please to mention my school, which is St. Fidelis cause again like another average individual and did BCOM from Aligarh Muslim University. I also had, during my school days, thousands of memories, and didn't cry when we left the school, because I have been so emotionally strong. This is something you can consider more than an ordinary individual could be.

And I would also like to mention my beloved mother Mrs. Rakhi Gupta, my husband Manish Agarwal, and my siblings Akash Goyal and Gagan Goyal for supporting me in my moments of happiness and sadness. These people broke the Iron curtains of the patriarchal society to comfort me so my growth doesn't get hampered by social evils.

Prologue

As we move forward as a culture, it's easy to leave behind the relics of the past. However, there are certain things that stand the test of time and preserve culture as they educate and entertain. These inspirational quotations are about life, happiness, and courage along with what we can learn from nature.

One of these art forms, which is given a relatively small amount of attention in modern society, is poetry and quotes.

It can be therapeutic for both its writers and its readers. It can give us advice about how to live and teach us important lessons about the past.

Through the skillful use of language, metaphor, and symbolism, poetry expresses human feelings in a way that day-to-day conversations don't.

Chapter One,

The Poetry

Life is a lot of work. What is it that gives us the strength to continue when we are tired and burned out? Sometimes an inspirational idea can help us renew ourselves and be filled with strength to fulfil our life's purpose. Inspiration comes in many forms. However, the root of all inspiration is the idea that our lives are meaningful. Inspiration is knowing that what I do matters deeply to the universe. When you have the feeling that your actions are meaningful, you will become filled with strength and vigour to fulfil your life's purpose.

Poetry should move us, make us think, and even make us laugh. But poetry can also inspire us and motivate us. Below, we introduce ten of the most inspirational and motivational poems ever written. These are poems that spur us to achieve great things, tell us we can make it, or encourage us to think big and be ambitious. I hope you find these poets' words inspirational!

Sir Edward Dyer, 'My Mind to Me a Kingdom Is'.

My mind to me a kingdom is;

Such present joys therein I find,

That it excels all other bliss

That earth affords or grows by kind:

Though much I want that most would have,

Yet still, my mind forbids me to crave ...

This poem has been popular with readers ever since it was first published in 1588 in William Byrd's Psalmes, Sonnets, & Songs. Yet the authorship of 'My mind to me a kingdom is' is by no means certain, and some anthologists now prefer to credit Edward de Vere, the Seventeenth Earl of Oxford, with authorship rather than Dyer. Whoever wrote it, it's an inspiring Renaissance poem about the power of 'mind over matter and the wonders of the human imagination.

Walt Whitman, 'Song of Myself.

I celebrate myself, and sing myself,

And what I assume you shall assume,

For every atom belonging to me as good belongs to you.

I loafe and invite my soul,

I lean and loafe at my ease observing a spear of summer grass

When Whitman's 1855 volume Leaves of Grass was published at Whitman's own expense – the first edition containing just a dozen untitled poems – even Whitman himself could have had little idea of the influence it would go on to have. Whitman would continue to revise and add to this collection throughout his life, and his exuberant free verse would go on to inspire French Vers libre as well as numerous fellow American writers.

'Song of Myself' is headed by Leaves of Grass, and it's a long and very inspirational opening poem. This statement of selfhood contains the famous line 'I am large, I contain multitudes. The link above takes you to several choice excerpts from the longer poem.

Emily Dickinson, '"Hope" is the Thing with Feathers.

As with many of her poems, Emily Dickinson takes an abstract feeling or idea and likens it to something physical, visible, and tangible. So hope becomes a singing bird. Hope, for Dickinson, sings its wordless tune and never stops singing it: nothing can faze it:

'Hope' is the thing with feathers –That perches in the soul –

And sings the tune without the words –

And never stops – at all –

W. E. Henley, 'Invictus'.

Out of the night that covers me,

Black as the pit from pole to pole,

I thank whatever gods may be

For my unconquerable soul.

In the fell clutch of circumstance

I have not winced nor cried aloud.

Under the bludgeonings of chance

My head is bloody but unbowed

Clint Eastwood's 2009 film about the 1995 Rugby World Cup in South Africa is named Invictus after this poem, and for good reason: Nelson Mandela recited the poem to his fellow prisoners while he was incarcerated on Robben Island. 'Invictus' was partly inspired by Henley's (pictured right) own struggles as an invalid (he lost a leg when young) and his determination to remain 'bloody but unbowed'.

The poem introduced a couple of famous phrases into the language: 'bloody, but unbowed', and the final two lines: 'I am the master of my fate: I am the captain of my soul.'

Rudyard Kipling, 'If—'.

If you can keep your head when all about you

Are losing theirs and blaming it on you,

If you can trust yourself when all men doubt you,

But make allowance for their doubting too;

If you can wait and not be tired by waiting,

Or being lied about, don't deal in lies,

Or being hated, don't give way to hating,

And yet don't look too good, nor talk too wise ...

Stoicism looms large in Kipling's famous poem – that is, the acknowledgment that, whilst you cannot always prevent bad things from happening to you, you can deal with them in a good way. This is summed up well in the reference to meeting with triumph and disaster and 'treat[ing] those two impostors just the same' – in other words, be magnanimous in victory and success (don't gloat or crow about it) and be dignified and noble in defeat or times of trouble (don't moan or throw your toys out of the pram).

A phrase that is often used in discussion or analysis of 'If—' is 'stiff upper lip', that shorthand for the typically English quality of reserve and stoicism in the face of disaster.

Max Ehrmann, 'Desiderata'.

This poem from the 1920s is a little different from others on this list, in that it's an example of the prose poem. Having drafted the poem in 1921 and registered it for copyright in 1927, Ehrmann then distributed the poem in a Christmas card in 1933.

A few years later, the psychiatrist Merrill Moore was given a copy of the poem, and he distributed 1,000 copies to his patients and soldiers during World War II. The poem thus became one of the great inspirational poetic messages of the twentieth century, particularly in the United States.

Langston Hughes, 'Dreams'.

In just eight short lines, probably the best-known poet of the Harlem Renaissance, Langston Hughes (1901-67), gives us words to live by –

reminding us that it's important to 'hold fast to your dreams because a life without them is a 'barren field'.

Philip Larkin, 'Coming'.

What, Philip Larkin, the poet who famously said that 'deprivation is for me what daffodils were for Wordsworth', appearing on a list of the most inspirational poems? But this quietly happy poem is arguable all the more inspiring and uplifting precisely because it is understated and written by a poet who isn't predominantly known for writing joyously about the world.

Here, Larkin reconnects with his childhood self as spring comes into view again, and he feels mysteriously happy.

Sylvia Plath, 'Ariel'.

Sylvia Plath – plagued by depression throughout much of her adult life, and eventually taking her own life in 1963 – may also seem an unlikely poet to find in a list of inspiring poems. But one of the most powerful ways that poets can inspire us is by taking their own personal suffering and showing how art can arise from it, and 'Ariel' is a beautiful example of this. This enigmatic poem uses the metaphor of an early morning horse ride to explore numerous shifting notions of identity.

The poem is often viewed as a reflection of Plath's early morning poetry-writing ritual in the months leading up to her death: she would wake, write poetry, and then spend the rest of the day employed in household chores. Read in this way, 'Ariel' can be understood as a powerful, if ambiguous, declaration of self-expression and freedom, albeit freedom desired rather than fully possessed. Nevertheless, the final image of Plath riding into the red dawn of the sunrise is inspirational in the extreme.

Maya Angelou, 'Phenomenal Woman.

Being a 'phenomenal woman' is not about being a certain size, or a particular shape. It's about how you carry yourself, and how you behave. As with several other classic Maya Angelou poems, 'Phenomenal Woman' is about being unbowed, holding one's head high, and being proud of who one is.

Ralph Waldo Emerson: Be Done With It

Finish every day and be done with it. You have done what you could;

Some blunders and absurdities no doubt crept in; Forget them as soon as you can

Tomorrow is a new day; You shall begin it well and serenely

And with too high a spirit; To be cumbered with your old nonsense.

Ella Wheeler Wilcox: I Will Be Worthy Of It

I may not reach the heights I seek,

My untried strength may fail me;

Or, halfway up the mountain peak

Fierce tempests may assail me.

But though that place I never gain,

Herein lies comfort for my pain —

I will be worthy of it.

I may not triumph in success,

Despite my earnest labor;

I may not grasp results that bless

The efforts of my neighbour

But though my goal I never see,

This thought shall always dwell with me—

I will be worthy of it.

The golden glory of Love's light

May never fall on my way;

My path may always lead through the night,

Like some deserted byway.

But though life's dearest joy I miss

There lies a nameless strength in this —

I will be worthy of it.

Charles R Skinner: Do it Now

If you have hard work to do, Do it now.

Today the skies are clear and blue,

Tomorrow clouds may come into view, Yesterday is not for you;

Do it now.

If you have a song to sing, Sing it now.

Let the notes of gladness ring

Clear as the song of a bird in Spring.

Let every day bring some music;

Sing it now.

If you have kind words to say, Say them now.

Tomorrow may not come your way,

Do a kindness while you may,

Loved ones will not always stay;

Say them now.

If you have a smile to show, Show it now.

Make hearts happy, roses grow,

Let the friends around you know

the love you have before they go;

Richard Watson Gilder:

He fails who climbs to power and place

Up the pathway of disgrace.

He fails not who makes truth his cause.

Nor bends to win the crowd's applause.

He fails not, he who stakes his all

Upon the right and dares to fall.

What though the living blesses or blame?

For him the long success of fame!

Chapter Two-

Prose.

The prose is a form of written or spoken language that typically exhibits a natural flow of speech and grammatical structure. A related narrative device is the stream of consciousness, which also flows naturally but is not concerned with syntax. The word "prose" first appeared in English in the 14th century. It is derived from the Old French prose, which in turn originates in the Latin expression prosa oratio (literally, straightforward or direct speech).

Works of philosophy, history, economics, etc., journalism, and most fiction (an exception is the verse novel), are examples of works written in prose. It differs from most traditional poetry, where the form has a regular structure, consisting of verse based on metre and rhyme. However, developments in twentieth-century literature, including free verse, concrete poetry, and prose poetry, have led to the idea of poetry and prose as two ends on a spectrum rather than firmly distinct from each other. The British poet T. S. Eliot noted that whereas "the distinction between verse and prose is clear, the distinction between poetry and prose is obscure.

Prose usually lacks the more formal metrical structure of the verses found in traditional poetry. It comprises full grammatical sentences (other than in stream of consciousness narrative), and paragraphs, whereas poetry often involves a metrical or rhyming scheme. Some works of prose make use of rhythm and verbal music. The verse is normally more systematic or formulaic, while prose is closer to both ordinary, and conversational speech.

In Molière's play Le Bourgeois gentilhomme, the character Monsieur Jourdain asked for something to be written in neither verse nor prose, to which a philosophy master replies: "there is no other way to express oneself than with prose or verse", for the simple reason that "everything that is not prose is verse, and everything that is not verse is prose".

- Dreams change you from what you are to what you want to.

Dreams take you to another edge of your life which you are now from what you want to be.

Dreams bring you to a more satisfied person in your life who you are and wish to be.

Dreams beautify your soul and what you are and wish to be in the future.

Dreams generate a different you.

Keep dreaming.

- We all have a right to write the right story for our life.

- It is always good to speak less and learn/listen/dream more which is the best medicine of our life.

- Don't let anyone's jealousy, hardness, ego, or negative attitude enter into your life against yourself. Instead, take them in a positive way so that you can show them your attitude which doesn't bother their behaviour.

- Don't design your character in such a way that everyone walks on it or design it like a sky that everyone desires to reach.

- The ways to succeed in life when you are positive, peaceful, and confident.

- As truly said by someone until we grow by ourselves, then only we can be a value to someone.

- Let's be vocal for local products along with starting and exploring our own creations.

- Make your own paintings, toys, dresses, applications, games etc. Be independent for yourself and for the country.

- Beginning is always the hardest and golden period of life.

- Never treat Anyone the way you don't want to be treated.

- Love life and love the ones around you.

- Any everlasting normal relation is better than a fake happy conditional relation.

- Being together always with flaws with no happiness is not fruitful. Instead happy, loving, truthful relationships are evergreen even though they do not last for a long time but give long term memories.

- Keep your promises and tell the truth.

- It's always better to tell people the truth up front. Don't play games with their feelings.

- People are real in reel life but not in real life, So be true, honest, and transparent.

- When your inner voice is with your ambitions and goals. then you can never stay behind in the same

- The only difference is beneath our society is that the poor people with low status don't have any recognition while the vice versa has a lot., we should think and change the tradition going on.

- Title - Time never remains the same.

I cried but it doesn't mean I haven't tried.

It seemed that clear sky was far away, and all hopes had washed away

But suddenly a ray of hope came and never had that much shame.

Known people forgot me but after having a courageous attitude they wanted to fall on their knees.

The Grass felt more greener and sky full of black clouds flew and got cleaner.

- Let's initiate small things everyone in which I was already on- make to do list which you thought of related to anything, talk to people whom you didn't get chance, work from home and work of home, planting, workout, reading, skill development for your cv, movies, medication, post your coolest pic, organise your cupboards and stuffs, plan your financials, things which you can improve ..

- Remember time is precious and so are you.

- You will be your own colour, but when you mix with other people that will create something new.

- I got hurt but he was broken.

- None can listen to your heartbreak unless they feel you.

- It's truly said by someone that you don't have to steal anything, instead you have to earn it.

- Your situations are nodes and the moments happening in them are lyrics which are creating a beautiful song in the form of life. So, make your song the way you want.

- Don't be so blind to understand your blood relations, evilness' and friend's care/love.

- If someone got more hurt than you that means he/she is totally into you.

- When you ignored, I understood the reason but when I ignored, you didn't get the same, that's called the gap of understanding.

- Opposite attracts in magnets but the truth is that the similarity takes people closer.

- Always remember karma always comes back to you in the same way.

- Karma is not a word rather it's a worse reality.

- Dear all women, never die a person inside you just because you are a beautiful woman in every way!!

- Never disgrace yourself from others taunts, intentions, and comments just because you are a courageous woman. Be proud of everything you have and go fearlessly wherever you want if you are correct and feel the same as you must take stand for yourself, and we all are with you.

- Your intention matters the most instead of your reaction.

- If you don't like doing something or talking to people, then don't do or talk as you will never be able to give your 100 percent but if you want to make the things happen then give 200 percent until you achieve.

- If you want to save your future, then gift plants instead of plucked flowers and plastic gifts.

- Always remember being like one when you leave this world, people will have tears for you not a sigh of satisfaction.

- We know good things and dreams are hard to achieve but trust God as it has its own journey which tastes good when in hand.

- It's more important to make your soul happy than anything else.

- Women have that universal power to make everything possible.

- If we can't behave like soldiers, then at least behave like good humans for the welfare of India, not like animals.

- This is the fact that you can laugh with many but cry with few.

- Your tears are reality to those who are closer to you.

- People who motivate others are real heroes for everyone's life.

- Make everyone's life bright instead of being a dark side for anyone.

- Might be your karma is not seen by one whom you want but it is being added to the list of God.

- The main satisfaction lies when you have peace in your soul, not a scream in the surrounding.

- Maybe you can delete memories of one whom you don't want from everywhere but not from heart ever.

- When we were kids, we needed everyone to hang on and to take care but when we grew up, we needed soul peace, happiness, and love to be within ourselves.

- There are a lot of things going on to improve India, but the reality is.

- We are not getting pure food at economical rates, affordable living, clean surroundings and at the end not the peaceful and happening life as in happiness index India is at the end but still it's incredible India.

- Do remember the quality of "clothes" and brand of "your name" really matters.

- You must be " you" if you want to make your dreams true as every time you can't be somebody else.

- Remember life is not an age or number it's an experience.

- Colours explain their identity in several situations and so your behaviour and attitude too.

- When I walk and roam around corners of several roads of my hometown.

- I found myself with the memories which I used to think of being in the future.

- You will always wonder if two types of people change during time.

- Ones who were born as caterpillars and grew to butterflies, others who were born as cacti and grew with only size. You decide which one you want to be.

- Do remember that your heart knows better than your brain.

- It's too strange that people are spending more on quality of looking rather than quality of living.

- Love should be eternal and should be like fragrance all over around.

- You can always grow and improve by natural things like exercise, being close to nature, growing plants rather than artificial stuff in tubes by companies.

- You must not lose a child from you till death.

- When I started, there were lots of obstacles but when I reached, I got to see my beautiful dream.

- You never know when the Universe can bring you more surprises in your life, so be ready for all with heart and mind.

- Love your nation who is giving you identity in everything and everywhere where you belong to HIND.

- Sometimes it's too late to make things right,

Sometimes we hurt others more than we realise.

Sometimes a Smile fades in front of our Eyes and

Sometimes we are the reason for tears in someone's eyes.

- It's natural that a person who exists on earth will leave one day. but never die a person inside you till the end.

- If you care for people and treat them well, then visiting religious places doesn't matter. God sees our intentions, efforts not ways to reach the place where scripture of God is kept.

- Just don't care what people think but do what your soul says.

- It's not always people who are the same but time, situation change everything.

- Love is meant to be natural, by heart. It's a feeling when you compromise for each other's happiness.

- I never understood this life journey well but the only thing I got to know very well is that life is meant to be a beautiful struggling story and if you are not struggling then you are dead.

- Every relationship has different phases.

- We come across many choices to choose but the decision should be the way we choose should be made unique and fruitful as any other choice could not be at the end.

• Yes, maybe we are bad for some people, but the beautiful thing is we are good for few and special for rare people.

• We don't know the results but what we should believe is on our hard work and what destiny has decided for us.

• It doesn't matter how your day went but what matters is how is your soul after spending that day.

• Often nowadays there are a lot of misunderstandings in relationships because instead of three basic needs i.e., love, care, and support, they focus more on three artificial words "I love you". So naturality is more important than artificiality which changes everything in relationships.

• Tears are more special and truthful than smiles. You know why because you can smile in front of everyone but can cry in front of few.

• Don't react over one incident so much as time changes and situations change.

• Investing time in yourself is best rather than wasting time on other useless things.

• A asked god. Me and B were good friends who studied in the same school, enjoyed being together. But why is B so successful after 20 years having millions and me earning lakhs.

GOD replied "When you were sleeping and having a relaxing time, B was making for opportunities to grow in future and slept for a few hours. "When you were travelling on holidays or with friends, B was working for his goals.

And that's how B is a millionaire, and you are part of that.

- With Independence Day coming, we are free India but are we still free to follow our dreams??

- I never failed because I always tried my best with self-trust.

- Yes, it is hard to set people on the right track as they love to fake and lie about their surroundings.

- Why don't we listen to our heart that can take us to heights instead of listening to others advice which can bury us.

- I know it's difficult to reach peaks but if it's impossible then I could have stopped. Hence, I will do my best every day.

- You know yourself far better than anyone else when you close your eyes and feel yourself for some moment.

- Your destiny depends on what you do, not what you think and speak.

- Spend time with yourself to analyse you as its biggest asset.

- Your happiness and sadness reflect with the people you live with. Thus, live with the people who make you happy, not sad. 99.99% Two zones i.e., GOD & parents can never think wrong for us even if situations are in front of us.so always think you are in 99% not in that 0.11 %.

- Never judge people on a few situations as they are going through many situations which make them like this.

- Always do remember ordinary people are many but extraordinary will be few.

- Your efforts fade when you allow darkness to enter over it.

- You can't change anyone because they do what their heart and brain say to do.

- How can anyone love and make you happy if that person can't keep his/her family happy.

- Girls, you are most beautiful for a person who sees you by heart but normal if he sees you by his brain.

- It's true that we can't be perfect but can be the closest to that.

- You are your own stems and roots as other people will come and go like wind, rain, storm but you must stay strong and stand against them.

- It's easy to say "it's OK" to someone but hard to forget the matter.

- Never judge others in conflict instead try to get into their story which they are going through.

- It's easy or hard on something to do as per your own capability of doing that.

- Never be so conscious or stressed on what you think instead focus on the reason for thinking that and come up with a solution on time.

- Life has been tough for all, but few bought outstanding results that they wanted while the majority got disheartened.

- The most audible voice you can hear is of yourself related to anything instead of anyone else.

- It's not about that people who are immature, irresponsible can never be good, but they need those rays which are already shone on almost perfect people by their inspirations.

- It's very important to have positive energy within yourself to yield the same instead of relying on bad energy to give positive results.

- Set your goals in which you can fail because when you achieve you will realise that you have done something which you can't.

- If you say you're going to do something, Do It!

If you say you're going to be somewhere, Be There!

If you say you feel something, Mean It!

If you can't, won't, and don't, then Don't Lie.

- Shame can bring you fame if you play a good game.

- Your extraordinary skills highlight the extraordinary tough time you had given to yourself.

- Never see back to progress instead see how many miles we can go.

- Optimistic people take out good in everything while pessimistic people bring out negativity out of positivity also.

- Our confidence, attitude and devotion decide our destiny.

- You are special with your own skills, attitude, and knowledge, so never compare yourself with others' cups of tea.

- Our reputed brand and success doesn't mean that we are great, instead it shows that we have tasted the ways of struggle and burnt ourselves for the glory which others couldn't have touched to that extent.

- If we don't value time thereon then at one point of time, it will let us know and realise its value.

- If life going easy that means we are far away from success.

- Never expect so much from others as the ultimate result is coming from our side.

- Never let anyone steal your glory.

- Imperfectness shows the level of perfection we can be one day or even more than that.

- Always learn that "you have to learn " always.

- Sacrifices and struggling takes you to the bright zone someday.

- The more you invest in yourself, the more you get in return afterwards.

- Don't distract from the obstacles you have on your journey, instead focus on your goal which will remove all those obstacles from your life.

- What matters most is how many people stay and understand you in your downfalls, not only in happenings.

- Your sight of positivity in every kind of negativity tells the dedication towards dreams and life.

- Never crush your dreams for your short-term pleasure because foremost one can make you king and latter one can make you janitor.

- It doesn't matter how many times you fall but what matters is how many times you get up to achieve your goal and rise.

- Wherever you invest but do with a good reason behind it.

- When the world seems so high, grab every opportunity to touch it, while when the world seems so low, grab every hand to hold that makes you feel high.

- Your compromises tell a type of person you are.

- Don't cry for ones who don't deserve you. Instead, be with those who try to see you all the time for any way by any way.

- You can make your own beautiful world surrounded by beautiful dreams that you dreamt of.

- Your name can do magic if you want to be done.

• Being close doesn't require daily conversation, love, or gestures. Instead, it just needs a feeling of understanding that we are not temporary but will remain forever.

• One who can understand your part before being told can understand your words in a better manner than anyone else could.

• Your ability to think can take you the way you want.

• In love emotional attachment is much more important than physical darkness.

• Your life is not restricted to your life only. It's like the connections that you have made with everyone around you.

• If you are a coward, then you have no option left of being dead in any way. But if you are courageous enough to think positive each time and have trust in yourself, then you are a winner at the end of your success.

• Good people or beautiful flower are some of living being which remains beautiful even after death

• Remember guys nothing is permanent and not a failure even not a success. So, remember your goal; your lovable ones and most importantly yourself.

• It's better to remain silent to close people than to complain. If we mean to them, they won't do it again and if not then they are not worth it to us.

- You can't get your words and actions right Back with you. So, react wisely.
- I never think I'm the best, but I try to be better every day.
- Being Successful is in your pocket if you have concern then u will use it and take care of it properly otherwise it will lose.
- Always be like a good flower because everyone wants to pass by and want to feel good fragrance not through the fragrance less flower.
- Don't fade your talent as it can be a beautiful fragrance one day.
- As the title of the book can't judge a book similarly a girl can't be judged by small things.
- You can make your words either like petals or like fire. As You can impress others or can be depressed.
- Be the follower of successors and failures both.
- If someone is there in your bad time and good time too, then that is the reality check of the people we live with.
- "If there is trust in love. .no matter how beautiful a man or a girl is in front. The one whom we love is only our PRINCE and PRINCESS.
- Help those who can't be helped by anyone easily because you are not helping that person only but doing God's work indirectly "
- You are only your success and failure depend on how you make it.

- Some people think they are rich because of money but the fact is people get rich because of their heart, nature, character, and words

- None can change any person, but love can change everything in person.

- Your success and efforts will surely be praised by everyone when it shines all over.

- We are equally sent by God but we ourselves create differences by our own efforts.

- Your availability on time will be understood by that person only who values your time.

- Don't try to please everyone, first please yourself and the ones who want to see you pleased.

- Cute relationships are when both are special for each other, and both are everything for each other.

- Many can live with your smile but only few will feel and understand your hidden tears.

- You can own anything by smiling/respect/helping but not by money.

- A smile can cover your tears but not your soul voice.

- Increase your face value up to that extent which will finally realise the meaning of your existence.

- Be an example for everyone instead of following others.

- Make yourself the most beautiful flower among all flowers in a simplest garden.

- Your success depends on what you think and do for it, not what others say.

- Start your days with dreams and end them with success.

- Problems in our life are living with wrong people and negative mind sets, not the situations. So, try to cut out the negativity and negative people by not destroying yourself.

- Many people may come and go but a key to remember for your life is give your life to that person who treats you and your family life more special than you.

- Once you have set your place in your mind and heart then no one can change it.

- Your life is like the way you see it.

- What you are and do today is your choice. What you were was your decision and what you will be is your will and dream.

- Be very sure while choosing someone as a reason for your happiness.

- People love to see us for what they want us for them not what we are for them.

- Your brain tells the way to walk, and the heart gives reasons to walk on that way.

- Real people in your life are only those who are with you and make you feel special when you stop loving yourself.

- One who truly loves you will accept you in a whole crowd and one who doesn't will not accept you even if you are too close to them. Be smart to know.

- Spend your time with those who are up to your expectations and love as you are giving that part of life which you won't receive back again.

- The beauty of success is that it comes to those who sacrifice their delightful things in life to make it beautiful.

- We are lucky if the one who makes us smile is the reason for our smile.

- One who can make you happy, can make you cry, being in love, and anger is closest among all.

- Ones who get affected by your everything, ones who will be there for you when you need them and ones who don't will be there for themselves only at the end.

- Treat others in a way as you want to be treated.

- You are only your strength and weakness

- Some love your smile,

Some love your face,

Some love your humour,

But the one who truly loves you truly will love everything in you.

- Be with ones who love you the way you are, who don't want to change you in any situations because those people will love your reality not your fake face to be accepted by all.

- Before finding out mistakes and imperfections in others. See yourself with your real sight and evaluate yourself first.

- Your life is not restricted to you. It's also a part of people who come, go, and creates more of it with you.

- If you like everyone that is your beauty and if someone doesn't like you that is their lack of beauty.

- Be in everyone's heart not in their brain.

- Your new life challenges give you the strength to work on your beautiful life more.

- It depends on you whether you want to stand on the green side or dark side of life.

- The people with whom we live are of our choice only.

- If you love yourself, then people will love you more.

- Your behaviour and character unveil the type of education and knowledge you had.

- The easy way of getting love is loving more of yourself but from the eyes of ones who don't want to change you for any reason.

- Don't be available for everyone but be special for the one who is not like everyone.

- Be different by making things different.

- When the world sees you wrong, prove yourself right.

- Make yourself smart enough instead dreaming of making smart surrounding.

- Add skills every day to be the best of your own.

- People don't break the promises, heart, and trust but they break that person who trusts them very closely.

- He said while smiling that I will allow you to go to anyone only if someone loves you more than me.

- It's difficult to leave people whom you get in love with and then they are not right for you.

Moral – use your brain with heart as when heart breaks, everything ends.

- Ones who say girls are confused and complicated are ones who don't understand their mom and sisters in their family and can't make them happy.

- 212- Everyone was looking at her, but she was looking at one and that's girls love.

- 213- Cut down the people who create trouble for you If they mean you. They won't create for long and if they don't then they won't ever solve.

- 214- Evergreen natural behaviour is more beautiful than fake changing seasons like behaviour.

- 215- Before thinking of ending any type of relationship just see and feel why you started those and why you are with them apart from your negative behaviour.

- Keep your tears safe only for ones who really know the worth of you and your smile.

- Be clear with your hearty words on time with people who spend your time. So that you won't regret and feel guilt when they are not part of your life as life is once and you mean to be happy in that.

- Always be your favourite

- Love people only till your heart allows and then let your brain speak to them.

- Never go on for someone's external beauty as it can change anytime but go for inner essence as it will intact you to live with them forever.

- Past is gone which is not going to be yours. Present is your intelligence what you can do and future is your dream world that you can build.

- If you want to earn, earn goodwill and money, do not be proud.

If you want to gain, gain power not enemies.

If you want to lose, lose bad deeds, not good people.

- Life is beautiful when we are with amazing people.

- Always believe in short loyalty instead of long term fakeness

- Plucked beautiful flower is a symbol of pain behind beauty.

- It's more important to be pretty from inside than external attractions.

- One who can do anything to save us from every dark side of the world is the most shining star for us.

- When someone can't wait for you, if you do each time then your value doesn't have any weight in that person's life so don't be in a basket of stupidity.

- People who see worth in you might go and will come back even if you don't want to. While those who don't value you will never come back even if you want.

Moral -let people go because your worth is more important than your desire.

- When you want to create in yourself, create good being in you and when you want to destroy something in you, destroy wrong deeds from your mind and heart.

- Strong real people will talk in front of you while fake coward people will enchanter behind you.

- If you want to see, to whom u matter then just stay silent in problems and the concerned and loving voices you will get in return will be your answer.

- She said what you see in my eyes he innocently replied, "I see my world in them ". He said and what you see in my eyes, she desperately looked and said "I see my life in them ". that's love.

- Ones who love us. can leave us for our happiness but can't hurt us in any way.

- It's better to be alone rather than being around fake people.

- Love has many colours like a rainbow although we can't feel that beauty every time but can feel it in every situation.

- Live with those who make your life worthy, not useless.

- Beautiful memories never get destroyed whether it's of past or present.

- Words of every Father -I kept you like a princess so I want you to be chosen for someone who can give you every happiness of life like a princess.

- Always be the preference and not a choice.

- There are some people who take our happiness for their happiness while some are happy in our happiness.

- Some people understand our silence while some even don't understand our words.

- Silence is the biggest and powerful tool to analyse and observe people in your life

- If people don't say things about you, it doesn't mean that they are not observing.

- Boys, no matter the way you see other girls, just think your mother was once a girl too.

- The Special one makes our favourite song our life.

- Money can't buy everything, if you are good enough in yourself and in everyone's heart then you have all edges of happiness on this earth.

- Love is not which can vanish like wind, but it's a strong stem which will stand firmly irrespective of many winds, storms, and rain.

- You are princess/prince of your kingdom if you treat your parents as king and Queen of your kingdom. It's only "you " who must uplift your quality of life, if you don't want to.

- Hard work needs reflection, not words to reflect it.

- The moment we start analysing our wrong, from then only we are one of the great people on earth.

- None is bad. It's just that everyone is not made for each other.

- Before doing wrong always remember people and God will always stand for your good not for bad deeds.

- Somebody who can fight for us from everyone is right for us.

- If someone is letting us down It means we are above them.

- Never hate ones who are jealous of you because they are ones who think you are better than them

- Sometimes behind a beautiful smile, there may be hidden heart-breaking tears.

- As we people need oxygen; water; food to live similarly any relation need understanding; trust and love to live happily forever

- It's useless when you care for someone more than yourself and that person loves himself/herself more than anyone else.

- Expect less from others and gain more.

- Fall in love with the right person so as not to make your whole life wrong.

- Always be careful while speaking harsh words in adverse time because,

- You can't take your words back and can't fix the broken heart back as before.

- Don't forget all the good things just because of one mistake.

- When someone shares something with you then always stand yourself in the other's position because at some moment of life, you can't even get the one to share with.

- One who wants us will show their presence from time to time and one who loves us will not give a chance of absence ever.

- It's true that many girls can hide their feelings and many boys can't express their tears.

- Never change and regret being good to others as one day they will realise that they were not of your standard and worth for you.

- Never cry for one's who can't understand you at that time because they don't value your smile either.

- Be the one who can win everyone's heart, not the one who can give heart to everyone.

- All we need is to feel every colour around us to reflect every colour of life.

- Our eyes are the worst enemy of our secrets.

- Don't think of others' silence as stupidity to not analyse you.

- If our heart is hurt by someone then it means that it has felt special too.

• If a temporary smile can make a snap good, then why don't we always smile by heart in every situation to make our life beautiful.

• IF

You hate someone, tell them the reason.

You love someone, tell them about their value in your life and place which no one can give.

You don't care, tell them that your time is more precious than them.

Don't complicate life otherwise life will complicate you!!

• Start living for your dreams instead of only imagining them.

• Although dream is just a 5-letter word, it takes all hard work for 5 organs to achieve that.

• Live your life to the fullest by your heart.

• We will come across many people in life, some will give us special life, and some will take it.

• If someone is available for you whenever you require them. It doesn't mean they are free, that means they value you more than their time.

• God couldn't come with us here, so he sent family for us so just love your family.

• Being a girl and taking a stand for yourself is itself a success and proud in this world. We struggle and adjust ourselves through different phases i.e., pain; conditions; challenges; people; time; still at last we prove ourselves that we are no more less than boys.

- We all are brave; beautiful so don't care what others say.

- Many people asked what you want to become. Although the fake answer was a successful one, inside the real voice was saying to be a kid again.

- Most heart touching: loving and true line said by loving ones that "Take care of yourself not for you but for myself"

- Memories with pics are more beautiful than memories with people. as people change but pictures remain beautiful forever.

- Save resources of earth otherwise, in meantime it will destroy its destroyers.

- Nature is the best example of our inner behaviour which never remains the same.

- Exercise is the best therapy for being fit and so is the conversation in any relationship.

- Many people may come and go but some remain forever.

- Make your life's movie real and interesting instead of watching fake interesting stories come up by people.

- Reality is bitter but bitter things are always healthy for us.

• Best example and reality is that we value things or people only when it becomes difficult to reach them like people wish to go to the stars; moon by destroying land; air; water who care for them all time.

• No relation can exist if you don't have mutual understanding; trust, love; and at last, a beautiful life with happiness all around.

• Some people hurt us badly, some love us badly while the first one shows our mistakes that we must not repeat and the latter one shows our beautiful life that we have with those people.

• Reality of people seems when they do what they said earlier.

• Observe people's real actions and reactions for you, not fake words said by them for us.

• When your desire for someone or something is true then the whole universe will give it to you.

• No one can think that a bit of theirs can make anyone's big day in their life's happiness .

• If time is more but memories are less then make sure to clear everything with everyone else words would be less and hope would be more.

• Social people have many choices but local people have choices.

• Maybe a lot of people said that they are with us, but it would feel special to be the one only whom we really want to be with.

- If you want good people in your life then first be a good person otherwise you will remain the same and that person leaving you will be in another person's good life.

- A green leaf does also shed one day as so is everything in our life.

- Your level of thinking can make u fly as beyond as u want n can Burry as down u can't think.

- First be yourself like the people you want in your life

- Don't live the way others live the way you like so that people would imitate your way of living to live their life.

- Before pointing others, first see yourself in mirror that how much you are perfect in yourself

- Don't give your happiness in anyone's hand.

- Put your best in everything and then let it be destiny where it takes.

- Give time to those who make it beautiful, not worthless.

- Get in love with those who love you more than you do to yourself because they will make your life more happening than you do.

- Instead hating people whom you don't like start loving yourself more

- Don't forget your diamonds of life while collecting worthless and temporary stones.

• Always remember the wealthiest tree would bend down and shower more irrespective of getting anything in return and so we should be.

• Leave people who don't know your reason for hurting them because this shows that they are dealing with the brain not following the relation by heart.

• There are few things to be happy forever.

Always give 1 compliment to any person.

Always be thankful for the people who were with you in difficulties.

Always give respect to those you matter to you the most.

Always do something grateful each day.

Always be the people who love you the most each day

• Some people who leave gave lesson for life and some memories for life.

• People are the only reason who give chances of ignorance and stay away from them.

• Sometimes people value us when we leave them.

• One who can listen to your heart is really a one who can see your dreams too.

• One who can recover you apart from a doctor is someone who deserves to be in your life always.

- If you feel the happiness of someone, then you will feel their pain too.

- Respect is a very short word but a great reflection of our behaviour.

- The best way to love people is to love their goodness instead of finding the dark side.

- Each moment brings out different plans to our life.

- It is not true that planned things go per plan so do always keep a backup.

- Make your relations with colours and put colours in relation.

- Moments are not perfect but make them from nice to wow.

- Live each day; living for people whom you love so that when you die; they can die each moment remembering each day they lived with you.

- Always value each person in your life because a single key can't unlock all problems and happiness in your life.

- Never see any person low because even a dead watch shows correct time twice a day.

- Sky and everything was the same, but people were different with different looks, nature, pursuing careers and that's the beauty of the universe, how everything works.

- Never show your weakness to the ones who can make their strength instead disclose to the ones who can change it to strength.

- Some people make our life special and leave and some make it hell and still exist.

- If you do bad for someone, do remember you will be only first victim by your deeds

- If you are living only for yourself, just imagine you are worthless even if you can't be compared to animals too.

- Animals are the best friends on the planet.

- If you can't be happy for others happiness, then don't expect others to care for you in hard times.

- One drop can't do anything when we are thirsty, same as one man (Prime Minister) can't do anything alone to improve our nation. We must fight all together and make this as one of the developed countries like others so that we can proudly say that we are part of it.

- Find solutions to problems. rather finding problems in everything.

- Educated people implement things and uneducated ones impose.

- Colours can let you feel beauty and living with those colours can make life beautifully complete.

- See beauty in everyone's soul, not imperfections. as nobody and nothing can't be perfect but can be beautifully complete.

- Although we can't own every heart. but by winning them; We can live in everyone's heart and can make ours.

- See possibility of things rather than its impossibility of doing it.

- Your dreams must be high not other's opinion on you.

- Dreams are not what we see while sleeping instead they are those which don't let us sleep.

- God gifted us so many unlimited luxuries with beautiful life, can't we give our trust upon him?

- A beautiful heart would always be a pure one, but a pretty face might have fakeness inside.

- God made us and we made differences

- If you don't love and live for yourself then why would others too.

- Be unique like a cherry, not a common piece of cake.

- Don't love things more than people because when you leave this world, people will cry not things.

- Everyone sees pain which thorns give to us while plucking beautiful roses but not its protection and love for rose.

- If you want to change anything and anyone, first change yourself to good habits to change the world.

- It's very easy to forgive anyone for their happiness but too difficult for our happiness.

- How strange Natural resources are giving us life and we are killing them though having God gifted brains.

- God has sent us like white paper with colours now it's on us to make it beautiful painting or rubbish with useless meaning.

- Be like one so that everyone wants you not like you want everyone.

- Money can't buy something, but your good soul can attract anything.

- If someone hurts, you are twice; thrice. let them do and forgive them because weaker people always do negative things and big people are always famous for their sacrifices and good deeds equal to God.

- Beautiful life is the prediction of blank life only by us.

- Eyes Depict best of everything, although they can't speak but they can tell everything.

- If you want to...

live; live happiness!!

Accept; accept truth!!

See; see reality even if it's bitter!!!

Feel; feel the beauty of everything and everyone!!

Do; apologize, care, sacrifice, love!!

Taste; taste colours of nature!!

Love; love yourself first n den everyone!!!

Hate, hate your selfishness!!

Make; make yours and everyone's world beautiful!!

Tell; tell d change that can be brought in anything n in anyone!!!!

Ask; ask reasons!

Save; save goodness!!

Invent; invent yourself!!

Learn; learn to feel guilty in apologising!!

Read; read truth!!

Erase; erase anger, jealousy, hateness among people!!

Serve; serve someone who needs us!!!

Explain; explain solutions!

Teach; teach them to save and inherent good deeds in this adorable world.

Lastly, if you want to be someone, be good in your eyes first.

- Fragrances are different but purpose is same, similarly, parents' nature is different, but purpose is same to nourish children.

- Some people need to be missed in their absence while some must be missed off from life to make it better.

- Sweetest part in life is to carry all the memories in life but the toughest part is to say goodbye to the person who is behind those memories.

- It matters how you see or judge others because it will show what you are not what you see which is exactly as a mirror.

- One who can change friendships and relationships can change your thinking too, to increase the gap from them!!

- Best friends are the ones who can make you cry from laughing too hard!

- Sometimes Your Heart Needs More Time to Accept What Your Mind Already Knows...!!!

- Life shows what you are, what you can do. It doesn't matter how many times you lose or you win. It gives you the way to think and experience everything, so be aware of the obstacles as they can also become part of your experiencing life and try to gain the flowers of happiness, so that you blossom everywhere and spread fragrance to yourself and to others too.

- If you shed tears when you miss the sun then you would also miss the stars too.

- You hurt me more than I deserve, is it just because I loved you more than you deserve?

- The seeds you are sowing today will surely reap one day. So do your best, think the best and be the best one.

- Always be inspirer, get better and better each day and love the way you are

- Your smile cost nothing to you but might be everything for someone

- Life has no end for one's who always understand the twists and turns but the ones who get herself/himself into it, end forever.

- You are your own creation at the end. so, utilise to make it as wonderful as you dream

- A mother is a wonderful human being in our life who gives part of her own to us for such a long time.

- It doesn't matter how hard the way is but matters how beautifully you reach your destination.

- When you make someone cry, all feelings of that person are lost and worry!!

When you make someone broken, that person's heart gets fully shaken!!

When we make someone happy by heart then that moment would be their life's part!!

so, to make every moment special in every special life for some people, we are at their first sight and last sight and feel too to be in their happiness!!!

- You never know how long people are with you so just ignore the three-letter word called "EGO" which can spoil more than 3 letter word relations.

- It's all about how you let yourself go into deeper roots by being independent, so that you can't be harmed by anyone else.

- A genius person never gives up irrespective of any obstacles.

- Live or at least make an effort to have a king size life else you will fall into king size worries.

- You are the best person yourself to expect and get everything which you want.

- You are the happiest person when you love with less burden of sorrows, past and more of happiness with a smile all the time as life is once and temporary.

- If you hurt a pure soul, then you will be a victim one day.

- When we lie or do something wrong then always remember even if nobody is watching but one always does.

- Just be good while thinking about others or don't care as you never know when God will take your bad vibes to yourself only.

- Even if you have grown up having hefty money with all luxuries around but you shod never forget your roots which were the reason of growth.

- A six-letter word is almost everything for us. His Sacrifice, love, care, concern, protection and Afterall to see his children growing everywhere. Do respect as you are lucky that you have image of God on earth

- If you are not a good brand as a person, then no other branded stuff will be worthy of your fake/mean or selfish personality.

- Always remember KARMA always comes back as if you use people for your happiness then God will use your happiness for other people.

- As today is a remarkable fashion Era but the major point between all is that your fashion sense first should match with your intellectual and confidence too as it represents what you are.

- Always make your personality as your fashion sense then everything will come into place.

- The people who are more interested in others' life and events never grow in the way they should be. So, focus on yourself first

- Yes, competition is too much in today's world. Maybe because we girls have exceptionally created the same. Go ahead Girls.

- If you don't allow the girls to let them do what they want then you are not stopping then, you are hiding talent from the welcoming world which she has.

- Sweetest part in life is to carry all memories but the toughest part is to say goodbye to the person who is behind these memories.

- Hard times reveal good friends.

- Men have the toughest souls to read as they don't express what they have inside.

- You can't change people, but you can change the people around you.

- We are always busy finding peace in other things but the real one is within us only.

- When you realise that your presence is temporary and should be fruitful then you start doing what needs to be done.

- People don't understand the value of relationships, feelings, money, lifestyle, right person in life etc until they feel and experience it.

- You are the best source of happiness in your life. Live with your own rules as it once was.

- Yes, I agree life is the same for all but not the lifestyle and dreams.

- Some people die as they are tired of fulfilling responsibilities while some give their luxury life to their grandchildren as well.

- Make sure people are jealous of your happiness, success, money, etc. Make them more jealous as the rising sun is always burning.

- Some people say you are lucky, but the fact is I made myself lucky through my efforts.

- People will come on your deathbed with good wishes if you have done something for them selflessly. In addition, people will come but not electronic devices.

- Love has no voice or gesture.

- Relations sustain for a long time which is followed with respect, heart, and devotion but not with the brain.

- No matter what people must give/take respect, love, and care in the relationship they are.

- Many relations to like and lots of tears to wipe.

Many Conversations to share and lots of memories to cheer.

Many things to hear and lots of clothes to wear.

Time is less precious and life is so gracious.

So have a quick call and recall all.

- Your personality should be impressive even on the dark side only.

- Never let your past scars overcome your upcoming beautiful life and way.

- Some things or people don't need to say about their beauty and belief, it's just reflected through them.

• People will judge you by your looks, way you take, knowledge, etc but you exactly know what to improve in yourself.

• Many of us know and understand the journey of the Mother who keeps us months in the womb but very few understand the journey of Father who keeps the child protected forever from everyone by anyway.

• You should own your thoughts, actions to recognize yourself in your own eyes.

• People need peace, positive thoughts, good people around and everything you want will come in place.

• Peace is everything.

• Always try your best to get whatever you like; else you will be forced to like whatever you get.

• As every song needs a good singer, so do our lives too to make it beautiful and worthwhile.

• A beautiful truth, poor people can have big dreams and make themselves successful while on the other hand rich people can make their life hell or worst

• Never give advice to someone until it's asked for as it won't have value.

• A ray of hope is someone's life turning point.

• Always be like a free bird.

- Be with someone who will look into your eyes and tell you how you are feeling.
- First, we must analyze and believe in ourselves instead of others.
- Life is also like a boat where we are balancing things and people and one who can't handle, gets drowned in water.
- Your success and being grounded go hand in hand and if not, then the time will bring you down
- Never waste stuff that keeps you alive i.e., food, water, and plants as they themselves are alive.
- Problems never see the beauty of a person so be with the person who can take away your worries and not the beauty of your life.
- We all know a lot, but the reality is nothing as God knows everything.
- Your life should be your favourite song.
- Be evergreened to be forever.
- It takes time to build but seconds to erase.
- Self- doubt is the best blame that anybody has.
- Everything around nature is the best example of discipline.
- The Surroundings could be the same but perspective could be different.

- We know who we are, but we never thought about what we can be.

- Winners never die but cowards do it themselves too many times.

- World is like a stage where you perform every other day and win or lose.

- Everything which shines is not gold so be aware.

- Your calmness reflects what you have gone through or experienced.

- You will take and give memories/fame/respect when you die not money.

- Self-reality check is the best test that we can do for ourselves.

- Life never stops until you give it a break.

- We can glare, or we can flare.

We can shine, or we can decline.

We can smile, or we can rule.

We can be winners, or we can be losers.

Chapter Three: Motivational Short Stories

The great thing about them is that they're so easy to digest, and there's always a moral at the end of the story.

Whether they're true stories or not is another thing, as many of them are legends supposedly hundreds of years old.

However, the stories that I'm talking about are so powerful and inspirational that many of them really do get you thinking and even leave you speechless at times.

Three Feet From Gold:

During the gold rush, a man who had been mining in Colorado for several months quit his job, as he hadn't struck gold yet and the work was becoming tiresome. He sold his equipment to another man who resumed mining where it had been left off.

The new miner was advised by his engineer that there was gold only three feet away from where the first miner stopped digging.

The engineer was right, which means the first miner was a mere three feet away from striking gold before he quit.

The Moral:

When things start to get hard, try to persevere through adversity.

Many people give up on following their dreams because the work becomes too difficult, tedious, or tiresome—but often, you're closer to the finish line than you may think, and if you push just a little harder, you will succeed.

Rocks, Pebbles, and Sand:

A philosophy professor once stood up before his class with a large empty mayonnaise jar. He filled the jar to the top with large rocks and asked his students if the jar was full.

His students all agreed the jar was full.

He then added small pebbles to the jar, and gave the jar a bit of a shake so the pebbles could disperse themselves among the larger rocks. Then he asked again, "Is the jar full now?"

The students agreed thatthe jar was still full.

The professor then poured sand into the jar to fill up all the remaining empty space.

The students then agreed again that the jar was full.

The Metaphor

In this story, the jar represents your life and the rocks, pebbles, and sand are the things that fill up your life.

The rocks represent the most important projects and things you have going on, such as spending time with your family and maintaining proper health. This means that if the pebbles and the sand were lost, the jar would still be full andyour life would still have meaning.

The pebbles represent the things in your life that matter, but that you could live without.

The pebbles are certain things that give your life meaning (such as your job, house, hobbies, and friendships), but they are not critical for you to have a meaningful life.

These things often come and go, and are not permanent or essential to your overall well-being.

Finally, the sand represents the remaining filler things in your life and material possessions. This could be small things such as watching television, browsing through your favorite social media site, or running errands.

These things don't mean much to your life as a whole, and are likely only done to waste time or get small tasks accomplished.

The Moral

The metaphor here is that if you start with putting sand into the jar, you will not have room for rocks or pebbles.

This holds true with the things you let into your life. If you spend all of your time on the small and insignificant things, you will run out of room for the things that are actually important.

In order to have a more effective and efficient life, pay attention to the "rocks," because they are critical to your long-term well-being.

The Elephant Rope (Belief)

A gentleman was walking through an elephant camp, and he spotted that the elephants weren't being kept in cages or held by the use of chains.

All that was **holding them back** from escaping the camp, was a small piece of rope tied to one of their legs.

As the man gazed upon the elephants, he was completely confused as to why the elephants didn't just use their strength to break the rope and escape the camp. They could easily have done so, but instead, they didn't try to at all.

Curious and wanting to know the answer, he asked a trainer nearby why the elephants were just standing there and never tried to escape.

The trainer replied;

"When they are very young and much smaller we use the same size rope to tie them and, at that age, it's enough to hold them. As they grow up, they are conditioned to believe they cannot break away. They believe the rope can still hold them, so they never try to break free."

The only reason that the elephants weren't breaking free and escaping from the camp was that over time they adopted the belief that it just wasn't possible.

Moral of the story:

No matter how much the world tries to hold you back, always continue with the belief that what you want to achieve is possible. Believing you can become successful is the most important step in actually achieving it.

Thinking Out of the Box (Creative

Thinking)

In a small Italian town, hundreds of years ago, a small business owner owed a large sum of money to a loan-shark. The loan-shark was a very old, unattractive looking guy that just so happened to fancy the business owner's daughter.

He decided to offer the businessman a deal that would completely wipe out the debt he owed him. However, the catch was that we would only wipe out the debt if he could marry the businessman's daughter.

Needless to say, this proposal was met with a look of disgust.

The loan-shark said that he would place two pebbles into a bag, one white and one black.

The daughter would then have to reach into the bag and pick out a pebble. If it was black, the debt would be wiped, but the loan-shark would then marry her. If it was white, the debt would also be wiped, but the daughter wouldn't have to marry the loan-shark.

Standing on a pebble-strewn path in the businessman's garden, the loan-shark bent over and picked up two pebbles.

Whilst he was picking them up, the daughter noticed that he'd **picked up two black pebbles** and placed them both into the bag.

He then asked the daughter to reach into the bag and pick one.

The daughter naturally had three choices as to what she could have done:

1. Refuse to pick a pebble from the bag.
2. Take both pebbles out of the bag and expose the loan-shark for cheating.
3. Pick a pebble from the bag fully well knowing it was black and sacrifice herself for her father's freedom.

She drew out a pebble from the bag, and before looking at it 'accidentally' dropped it into the midst of the other pebbles. She said to the loan-shark;

"Oh, how clumsy of me. Never mind, if you look into the bag for the one that is left, you will be able to tell which pebble I picked."

The pebble left in the bag is obviously black, and seeing as the loan-shark didn't want to be exposed, he had to play along as if the pebble the daughter dropped was white, and clear her father's debt.

Moral of the story:

It's always possible to **overcome a tough situation** throughout of the box thinking, and not give in to the only options you think you have to pick from.

The Group of Frogs (Encouragement)

As a group of frogs was traveling through the woods, two of them fell into a deep pit. When the other frogs crowded around the pit and saw how deep it was, they told the two frogs that there was no hope left for them.

However, the two frogs decided to ignore what the others were saying and they proceeded to **try and jump out of the pit.**

Despite their efforts, the group of frogs at the top of the pit were still saying that they should just give up. That they would never make it out.

Eventually, one of the frogs took heed to what the others were saying and he gave up, falling down to his death. The other frog continued to jump as hard as he could. Again, the crowd of frogs yelled at him to stop the pain and just die.

He jumped even harder and finally made it out. When he got out, the other frogs said, **"Did you not hear us?"**

The frog explained to them that he was deaf. He thought **they were encouraging him** the entire time.

Moral of the story:

People's words can have a big effect on other's lives. Think about what you say before it comes out of your mouth. It might just be the difference between life and death.

A Pound of Butter (Honesty)

There was a farmer who sold a pound of butter to a baker. One day the baker decided to weigh the butter to see if he was getting the right amount, which he wasn't. Angry about this, he took the farmer to court.

The judge asked the farmer if he was using any measure to weight the butter. The farmer replied, "Honor, I am primitive. I don't have a proper measure, but I do have a scale."

The judge asked, "Then how do you weigh the butter?"

The farmer replied;

"Your Honor, long before the baker started buying butter from me, I have been buying a pound loaf of bread from him. Every day when the baker brings the bread, I put it on the scale and give him the same weight in butter. If anyone is to be blamed, it is the baker."

Moral of the story:

In life, you get what you give. Don't try to cheat others.

The Obstacle In Our Path (Opportunity)

in ancient times, a King had a boulder placed on a roadway. He then hid himself and watched to see if anyone would move the boulder out of the way. Some of the king's wealthiest merchants and courtiers came by and simply walked around it.

Many people loudly blamed the King for not keeping the roads clear, but none of them did anything about getting the stone out of the way.

A peasant then came along carrying a load of vegetables. Upon approaching the boulder, the peasant laid down his burden and tried to push the stone out of the road. After much pushing and straining, he finally succeeded.

After the peasant went back to pick up his vegetables, he noticed a purse lying in the road where the boulder had been.

The purse contained many gold coins and a note from the King explaining that the gold was for the person who removed the boulder from the roadway.

Moral of the story:

Every obstacle we come across in life gives us an opportunity to improve our circumstances, and whilst the lazy complain, the others are creating opportunities through their kind hearts, generosity, and willingness to get things done.

The Butterfly (Struggles)

A man found a cocoon of a butterfly.

One day a small opening appeared. He sat and watched the butterfly for several hours as it struggled to force its body through that little hole.

Until it **suddenly stopped making any progress** and looked like it was stuck.

So the man decided to help the butterfly. He took a pair of scissors and snipped off the remaining bit of the cocoon. The butterfly then emerged easily, although it had a swollen body and small, shriveled wings.

The man didn't think anything of it and sat there waiting for the wings to enlarge to support the butterfly. But that didn't happen. The butterfly spent the rest of its life unable to fly, crawling around with tiny wings and a swollen body.

Despite the **kind heart of the man**, he didn't understand that the restricting cocoon and the struggle needed by the butterfly to get itself through the small opening; were God's way of forcing fluid from the body of the butterfly into its wings. To prepare itself for flying once it was out of the cocoon.

Moral of the story:

Our struggles in life develop our strengths. Without struggles, we never grow and never get stronger, so it's important for us to tackle challenges on our own, and not be relying on help from others.

Control Your Temper (Anger)

There once was a little boy who had a very bad temper. His father decided to hand him a bag of nails and said that every time the boy lost his temper, he had to hammer a nail into the fence.

On the first day, the boy hammered **37 nails** into that fence.

The boy gradually began to control his temper over the next few weeks, and the number of nails he was hammering into the fence slowly decreased.

He discovered it was easier to control his temper than to hammer those nails into the fence.

Finally, the day came when the boy didn't lose his temper at all. He told his father the news and the father suggested that the boy should now pull out a nail every day he kept his temper under control.

The days passed and the young boy was finally able to tell his father that all the nails were gone. The father took his son by the hand and led him to the fence.

"you have done well, my son, but look at the holes in the fence. The fence will never be the same. When you say things in anger, they leave a scar just like this one. You can put a knife in a man and draw it out. It won't matter how many times you say I'm sorry, the wound is still there."

Moral of the story:

Control your anger, and don't say things to people in the heat of the moment, that you may later regret. Some things in life, you are unable to take back.

The Blind Girl (Change)

There was a blind girl who hated herself purely for the fact she was blind. The only person she didn't hate was her loving boyfriend, as he was always there for her. She said that if she could only see the world, she would marry him.

One day, someone donated a pair of eyes to her – **now she could see everything**, including her boyfriend. Her boyfriend asked her, "now that you can see the world, will you marry me?"

The girl was shocked when she saw that her boyfriend was blind too, and refused to marry him. Her boyfriend walked away in tears, and later wrote a letter to her saying:

"Just take care of my eyes dear."

Moral of the story:

When our circumstances change, so does our mind. Some people may not be able to see the way things were before, and might not be **able to appreciate them**. There are many things to take away from this story, not just one.

This is one of the inspirational short stories that left me speechless.

Puppies for Sale (Understanding)

A shop owner placed a sign above his door that said: "Puppies For Sale."

Signs like this always have a way of attracting young children, and to no surprise, a boy saw the sign and approached the owner;

"How much are you going to sell the puppies for?" *he asked.*

The store owner replied, "Anywhere from $30 to $50."

The little boy pulled out some change from his pocket. "I have $2.37," he said. "Can I please look at them?"

The shop owner smiled and whistled. Out of the kennel came Lady, who ran down the aisle of his shop followed by five teeny, tiny balls of fur.

One puppy was lagging considerably behind. Immediately the little boy singled out the lagging, limping puppy and said, "What's wrong with that little dog?"

The shop owner explained that the veterinarian had examined the little puppy and had discovered it didn't have a hip socket. It would always limp. It would always be lame.

The little boy became excited. "That is the puppy that I want to buy."

The shop owner said, "No, you don't want to buy that little dog. If you really want him, I'll just give him to you."

The little boy got quite upset. He looked straight into the store owner's eyes, pointing his finger, and said;

"I don't want you to give him to me. That little dog is worth every bit as much as all the other dogs and I'll pay full price. In fact, I'll give you $2.37 now, and 50 cents a month until I have him paid for."

The shop owner countered, "You really don't want to buy this little dog. He is never going to be able to run and jump and play with you like the other puppies."

To his surprise, the little boy reached down and rolled up his pant leg to reveal a badly twisted, crippled left leg supported by a big metal brace. He looked up at the shop owner and softly replied, "Well, I don't run so well myself, and the little puppy will need someone who understands!"

Box Full of Kisses (Love)

Some time ago, a man punished his 3-year-old daughter for wasting a roll of gold wrapping paper. Money was tight and he became infuriated when the child tried to decorate a box to put under the Christmas tree.

Nevertheless, the little girl brought the gift to her father the next morning and said, "This is for you, Daddy."

The man became embarrassed by his overreaction earlier, but his rage continue when he saw that the box was empty. He yelled at her; "Don't you know, when you give someone a present, there is supposed to be something inside?"

The little girl looked up at him with tears in her eyes and cried;

"Oh, Daddy, it's not empty at all. I blew kisses into the box. They're all for you, Daddy."

The father was crushed. He put his arms around his little girl, and he begged for her forgiveness.

Only a short time later, an accident took the life of the child.

Her father kept the gold box by his bed for many years and, whenever he was discouraged, he would take out an imaginary kiss and remember the love of the child who had put it there.

Moral of the story:

Love is the most precious gift in the world.

THE END

Contents

Printed by Libri Plureos GmbH in Hamburg,
Germany